BRINDISI

SUEZ

ADEN

BOMBAY

CALCUTTA

TO SINGAPORE

HONG KONG

YOKOHAMA

When Phileas Fogg bet his friends that he could travel right round the world in eighty days, he little knew how difficult it was going to be. This story tells of his many hair-raising adventures as he tried to win his bet.

Published by Ladybird Books Ltd Loughborough Leicestershire UK
Ladybird Books Inc Auburn Maine 04210 USA

© LADYBIRD BOOKS LTD MCMLXXXII

Printed in England (3)

AROUND THE WORLD IN EIGHTY DAYS

by Jules Verne

retold in simple language
by Joyce Faraday

illustrated by Kathie Layfield

Ladybird Books

Around the World in Eighty Days

Phileas Fogg was a man of mystery. Apart from a few simple facts, no one knew anything about him. He had no family and lived in a large house in London. He was rich but had only one servant to look after him.

Fogg was a man of very exact habits. In his house hung a time-table. It showed that he had tea and toast at exactly 8.23 each morning.

At 9.37 his servant took him his shaving-water heated to exactly 86° Fahrenheit. Each day, at exactly 11.30, he left home and went to the Reform Club.

He spent his day at the club reading. Then, at exactly 6.10, he played cards, and returned home afterwards at exactly the same time each evening. His fellow card-players found the handsome Phileas Fogg quiet and charming. They noted that he never seemed interested in money. Any money he won at cards he gave to charity.

Because these few simple facts were all that anyone knew about him, what began as a bet nearly ended in tragedy for Phileas Fogg. It happened like this. . . .

On the second day of October, 1872, a new servant went to work for Phileas Fogg. He was a Frenchman named Jean Passepartout. He had had many jobs. He had been a fireman in Paris, a singer, and an acrobat in a circus. He was strong, yet gentle, and his happy, smiling face made him popular wherever he went. After wandering from job to job, all Passepartout wanted now was to settle down and lead a quiet life. Phileas Fogg seemed to be just the master he needed – he couldn't have been more wrong!

At half-past eleven on the day Jean Passepartout started work, Phileas Fogg went, as usual, to the Reform Club. He spent the day reading, then at ten minutes past six, as usual, he met his friends for their game of cards. They were talking excitedly about a bank robbery – £55000 had just been stolen from the Bank of England. The thief had picked up a bundle of notes and simply walked out with them. Several people had seen him, and his description had been sent out. A reward was offered for his capture, and detectives were watching railway stations and ports to try to stop him leaving the country.

As they played, the card-players talked of hiding places where a bank-robber could lie

low. They wondered how quickly he could get abroad to escape the hunt.

'The world is a big place to hide in!' said one.

'Yes,' agreed Phileas Fogg, 'but now that we have telegrams, railways and steamships, the world has become much smaller.'

'The world hasn't shrunk,' replied one of his friends, 'just because we can travel around it in three months!'

'You don't need three months!' said Fogg. 'You can travel around the world in eighty days!'

'Eighty days! Impossible!' laughed another player.

'Think of the things that could go wrong!' said a third.

'No!' exclaimed Phileas Fogg. 'I know it can be done. I'll bet twenty thousand pounds on it. To prove it, I'll set out tonight! I shall go around the world in eighty days!'

'You're joking!' 'You can't leave tonight!' 'You'll never do it!' exclaimed his friends, one after the other.

'I will,' said Fogg quietly. 'An Englishman doesn't joke when he makes a bet like this. Do you accept the bet?'

'Very well,' his friends agreed, 'we accept.'

'Good,' Fogg told them. 'Today is Wednesday, October 2nd. I shall be back here, in the Reform Club, at a quarter to nine, on Saturday, December 21st. Now, gentlemen, let us finish our game!'

When he got home, Phileas Fogg called to his servant, 'Pack a small bag, Passepartout. We leave for Dover in ten minutes. We are going around the world.'

'Around the world!' gasped Passepartout.

'Yes, around the world,' Fogg repeated. 'We start at once!'

'A fine thing!' muttered poor Passepartout as he packed a bag. 'All I wanted was a quiet life! Now I've a master who sets out on a crazy adventure!'

By eight o'clock they were ready to leave. Fogg carried a time-table of the ships and railways of the world. Into their bag he slipped a thick roll of banknotes.

'Take good care of this bag,' he told Passepartout. 'It has twenty thousand pounds in it.'

At the station Fogg booked two tickets to Paris. His friends from the Reform Club were waiting to see him off.

'Gentlemen,' he said, 'when I return you may examine my passport. You will be able to

see the stamps of the countries I shall have passed through. They will prove I have been around the world. We will meet again at a quarter to nine on the evening of Saturday, December 21st.'

The train puffed out of the station. Phileas Fogg sat silently in his corner seat, and Passepartout, hugging the bag, stared out gloomily into the dark night.

The news of Phileas Fogg's bet spread like wildfire. His picture was in every newspaper, and people spoke of little else. Some thought he was bound on an exciting adventure, others shook their heads and said he must be mad.

Fogg and Passepartout travelled from Paris to Italy. There they went aboard the steamer, *Mongolia*, that would take them to Bombay, on the west coast of India.

At Suez, Passepartout, holding a passport, went ashore. A stranger, standing near the ship, watched him closely.

'Can I help you, sir?' the stranger asked Passepartout.

'I want to get this passport stamped,' Passepartout told him. 'Can you tell me the way to the Consul's office?'

The stranger's keen eyes studied the passport. In it he saw the picture of Phileas Fogg.

'This is not your passport,' he said. 'The owner of the passport will have to come ashore and go to the office himself.'

'That won't please my master,' said Passepartout. He hurried back on board to find Phileas Fogg.

The stranger hurried to the Consul's office.

'Sir,' he told the Consul, 'my name is Fix. I am a detective, sent here by Scotland Yard. We are searching for a bank-robber. I'm sure he has just arrived in Suez. You must keep him here until I can get a warrant for his arrest!'

'I can't do that,' said the Consul. 'If his passport is in order, I can't keep him here.'

Phileas Fogg walked into the office. Whilst the Consul stamped the passport, Fix stared at Fogg. He was sure this was his man! He mustn't let Fogg out of his sight! Before the ship sailed for Bombay, he would have to send a telegram to London.

That evening, a telegram arrived at Scotland Yard:

Suez to Scotland Yard, London.

HAVE FOUND BANK-ROBBER PHILEAS FOGG.
SEND WARRANT OF ARREST TO BOMBAY.

FIX, DETECTIVE.

Soon the newspapers were full of stories about the mystery man, Phileas Fogg. In the Reform Club, other members carefully examined his photograph. It was certainly very like the description of the bank-robber! His world tour was just a trick to throw the police off his track. Instead of being a hero, Fogg was now a hunted bank-robber!

On board the *Mongolia*, Phileas Fogg played cards. Detective Fix was on board, too, and Passepartout was pleased to meet him again. Passepartout told him all about his rich master and his trip around the world. Everything the servant told him made Fix more and more sure that Fogg was the bank-robber. Of course, it never entered poor Passepartout's head that Fix was a detective hunting his master.

When they reached Bombay there were three hours to spare before the train left on its long journey across India to Calcutta. Passepartout set out to explore Bombay. He went into a temple. Three angry priests threw themselves on him, because he had entered their temple without taking off his shoes. Passepartout fought them off bravely and

escaped. At the railway station he told Fogg about the fight. Fix, still waiting for his arrest warrant, watched them and listened.

'If I could have Passepartout put in prison for fighting in the temple,' thought Fix, 'Fogg will have to wait for him to be set free. By then the arrest warrant will have come and I shall get my man!'

The train left and Fix stayed behind. He had work to do if Passepartout was to be arrested.

The train rolled steadily across India. Then suddenly, without warning, it stopped, and the startled passengers were told to get out.

'Look, sir!' cried Passepartout. 'There's no more railway track!'

The railway lines stopped fifty miles short of the next station! The passengers would have to make their own way there. Passepartout thought quickly, then ran to a nearby village. He soon returned with good news for his master. 'Sir,' he cried excitedly, 'I've found a man who has an elephant. He will take us to the next station!'

Soon they were bumping and bouncing along on the back of an elephant, on their way to Calcutta. After a while, they could hear strange sounds ahead. The driver halted the elephant to listen.

'Bandits!' said Passepartout.

They moved away from the path quietly, and hid among the trees to watch from a distance. A big funeral procession passed by, with drums beating and voices wailing. A Raja had died, and his body was being taken to be burned. His beautiful young wife, Aouda, was being led along by armed guards.

'What will happen to her?' asked Fogg.

'She will be burned alive, with the body of her dead husband,' whispered the driver.

'Never!' said Fogg. 'We must save her! Follow them!'

17

At a safe distance, they followed the procession. When it stopped near a temple, they waited once more among the trees. As they watched, a great pile of wood was stacked up for a fire, and the Raja's body was placed on top of it. Then, as night fell, the guards led the young wife into the temple. Guards stood around its walls.

In the darkness, Passepartout worked out a plan to rescue Aouda, and just before dawn, he crept silently to the fire. He climbed to the top and hid in the pile of logs.

As the rays of the morning sun filled the sky, the lovely Aouda, fainting with fear, was led by the guards to the funeral fire. The guards forced her to lie down beside her dead husband. Wild singing broke out from the great crowd, and the drums began to beat once more. Then, the fire was lit. Flames and smoke shot up to the sky. Knife in hand, Phileas Fogg was about to dash forward when suddenly, out of the flames and smoke, Passepartout stood up on top of the fire. Terrified, the guards and mourners threw themselves to the ground. 'The Raja lives!' someone cried.

Passepartout seized Aouda from the flames,
bounded from the fire, and dashed with her to
safety. Phileas Fogg helped them onto the
elephant, and they were off. Shots and cries
rang out behind them. They had escaped in
the nick of time! As the elephant moved
swiftly over the ground, away from danger,
Aouda thanked her rescuers. Her beautiful
eyes were filled with tears of joy.

That night they reached the next railway
station, and boarded the train for Calcutta.
Fogg had been thinking hard, and he knew
that Aouda would never be safe in India. He
had decided to take her with him to Hong
Kong, where she had a cousin who would
take care of her. But when they got out of the
train at Calcutta, a policeman stopped them.

'If I'm charged with stealing Aouda,' thought Fogg, 'I shall refuse to send her back to her death!' To his surprise, however, the policeman arrested Passepartout, and charged him with fighting in the temple in Bombay.

In the court, Fogg paid his servant's fine. At the back of the court-room, Fix, the detective, was furious. The arrest warrant for Fogg had still not arrived, and he could delay him no longer.

Just as the steamer for Hong Kong was about to sail, they all raced on board. During the voyage, Phileas Fogg and Aouda spent their time happily. He found her gentle and charming, and she learned to love the noble, kindly man who was taking her to safety.

Passepartout was surprised to see Fix again. He began to think he might be a spy sent by the Reform Club to watch them, but he did not tell Phileas Fogg of his suspicions.

Despite fierce storms, they docked in Hong Kong sixteen hours before their next ship, the *Carnatic*, sailed for Yokohama in Japan. Fogg hurried into town with Aouda, to find her cousin. To Aouda's dismay, however, her relative had left Hong Kong and had gone to live in Holland.

'You must come to Europe with us!' Phileas Fogg told her.

Meanwhile, Passepartout had wandered into the city on his own. Much to his surprise, he met Fix.

'Are you going to Japan, too, sir?' he asked.

'I am,' the detective told him. Together they went to book tickets for the ship to Yokohama. At the ticket office they learned that she would sail earlier than they had expected.

'My master will be pleased to sail tonight,' Passepartout said. 'I must hurry to tell him.'

'There's plenty of time,' said the cunning detective. 'Let's have a glass of wine together.'

Over a glass of wine, Fix at last told Passepartout that he was a detective. 'Your master,' he said, 'is the missing bank-robber. Help me to catch him and I'll share the reward with you!'

'Nonsense!' cried Passepartout. 'My master is the most honest of men! I'll never betray such a fine man! Never!'

'You know nothing about him,' Fix told the loyal Passepartout. 'But at least we can still be friends,' he went on. 'Come on, let's have another drink!'

Again they drank. Poor Passepartout's head began to reel. Fix placed a pipe in the servant's hand. Passepartout took a few puffs, not knowing that he was smoking a pipe of opium. In moments, he fell into a drugged sleep.

Quietly Fix slipped away. Now the *Carnatic* would sail without Fogg and his servant! If only the arrest warrant would arrive! Then the detective could arrest Phileas Fogg and the reward would be his!

Fogg and Aouda waited for Passepartout to return. When he did not come, they hurried to the docks. Passepartout was not there. Instead, they found Fix, who told them that the *Carnatic* had already sailed.

'In that case,' said Fogg, 'I shall find another ship to take us!'

The detective's heart sank. He was going to be unlucky again, because the warrant had still not arrived.

Fogg quickly found the captain of a small boat willing to take them to Shanghai. There they could catch a steamer for Yokohama. 'You have also missed the *Carnatic*,' Fogg said to Fix. 'May we take you with us?'

Fix gladly agreed. Thanks to the bank-robber's kindness, the detective could still keep an eye on him!

Fogg had the town searched for Passepartout but in vain. Fix kept silent. When the ship was ready to sail, Fogg and Aouda sadly had to leave without their faithful servant.

On the second day at sea they ran into bad weather, and a typhoon began to blow up. Soon great waves were crashing over the ship. Lashed by the typhoon, the ship creaked and rolled. Then, near the coast of China, the wind dropped. They had lost valuable time and were still a hundred miles from Shanghai. The captain ordered full steam ahead. Then, just as Shanghai came into sight, they saw a big steamer sailing towards them.

'We're too late!' the captain yelled. 'That's your ship for Yokohama!'

'Signal to her!' ordered Fogg.

The big steamer slowed, and the little ship pulled alongside her. Aouda, Phileas Fogg, and Fix climbed aboard. As they waved goodbye to the captain of the little ship, the steamer moved off on the journey to Yokohama.

'If only Passepartout were with us!' said Aouda.

What none of them knew was that Passepartout was already on his way to Japan, too. Although still sleepy from the opium Fix had given him, he had struggled to the docks. Sailors had carried him on board the *Carnatic* as she was about to sail.

They had put him in his cabin where he had fallen asleep. When he had recovered, he had searched for his master. Fogg and Aouda were not on board. He realised that Fix had tricked him, and he felt utterly miserable. It was his fault that his master had missed the boat. If Phileas Fogg failed to get to London on time and lost his bet, he, Passepartout, was to blame!

Alone and penniless, he stepped ashore in Yokohama. He wandered the streets, wondering how he could earn money to get back to London. Then a poster, in English, caught his eye. It read:

GRAND SHOW
CLOWNS!   ACROBATS!   JUGGLERS!
TONIGHT!

'The very thing!' he thought. 'I'll get a job as an acrobat!' And he went straight into the theatre.

'Yes, we can use a strong man,' said the leader of the acrobats. 'We need a man to hold up our Human Pyramid. You have to lie on your back, and the rest of us balance on top of you.'

At three o'clock the show began. With a roll of drums, fifty acrobats leapt onto the stage.

Passepartout lay down and the rest, climbing on each other, balanced on top of him. The crowd cheered and the band played as the Human Pyramid grew higher and higher. As he lay on his back, Passepartout could see up into the theatre. There, up in the gallery, he saw Mr Fogg and Aouda!

'Master!' shouted Passepartout joyfully. He pushed off the men on top of him, and the Human Pyramid collapsed in a heap. He raced off the stage to join his lost master and Aouda. The theatre was in uproar. The acrobats were wild with anger but Fogg, delighted to be with his servant again, calmed them with a handful of bank notes.

Together, the three made their way to the docks to board the steamer that would take them across the Pacific Ocean to America. Fogg told his servant how he, Aouda and Mr Fix had reached Japan. Passepartout told them he had missed them because he had been smoking opium. He did not mention his meeting with the detective.

The steamer sailed on time for San Francisco. 'So far, so good!' said Phileas Fogg. 'At this rate we will be back in the Reform Club in time!'

Passepartout was delighted. He was back with his master and Aouda. Mr Fogg could still win his bet and, at last, they seemed to be free of Fix. He was glad, too, that he had not told his master about the detective. Clearly, there had been a mistake, and there had been no need to worry him.

He was feeling his old, cheerful self as he went for a walk on deck, then, turning a corner, he came face to face with Fix! Without a word, he rushed at Fix, raining blows on him, and knocked him down.

'That's for the trick you played on me!' he roared. 'Any more of your tricks and I'll break your neck!'

Wisely, Fix kept out of sight for the rest of the voyage, and eleven days later the ship sailed into San Francisco.

That evening they were on the train for New York, three thousand seven hundred and eighty six miles away. In seven days the train

should take them from the Pacific to the Atlantic Ocean. They had eighteen days left.

All was going well, Fogg decided. To his surprise and delight, Mr Fix was also on the train. Passepartout was neither surprised nor delighted!

Through the night the train roared on, through the Rocky Mountains and over raging rivers. Then they were crossing the prairies. Suddenly the train stopped as thousands of great buffaloes charged across the railway track. For hours they passed in front of the train, like a brown river stretching as far as the eye could see.

Passepartout fumed at the delay, but nothing disturbed Phileas Fogg. He spent long hours playing cards, as if time did not matter! When at last the train moved on, snow began to fall. Passepartout grew worried again, for he knew that soon the prairies would be covered with snow. A heavy snowfall could block the track and end their adventure.

On the third morning, the train stopped suddenly again, and Passepartout went to see what was the matter.

'No, you can't cross the river,' he heard a signalman say. 'The bridge isn't strong enough

to take the train!'

The train driver was not to be stopped. 'Let me through!' he demanded. 'If we go at top speed we'll nearly fly across!'

He reversed the train down the track, then drove forward, quickly gathering speed. The engine shrieked. The train shuddered. They were doing sixty, eighty — a hundred miles an hour! The wheels hardly seemed to touch the track. They were over the river in a flash! As the last carriage reached the opposite bank, the bridge behind it crashed into the raging river.

The next day danger struck once more. Savage yells and rifle fire filled the air as a band of Sioux Indians attacked the train.

A hundred of them galloped beside it, and some leapt aboard. The rifle fire was answered by pistol shots from the passengers.

The Sioux Chief sprang from his horse onto the engine. He knocked out the engine-driver and his mate, then tried to stop the train by turning a wheel.

The engine roared on even faster. He had turned the wheel the wrong way!

'The train must be stopped!' cried Fogg, starting for the door.

'No, sir!' said Passepartout. 'Not you! I'll go!'

Unseen by the Indians, he got out of the carriage, then climbed along under the racing train. Clinging to the swinging chains, he worked his way forward until he reached the engine. Quickly, he set the engine free from the coaches, and they began to slow down.

As the coaches neared a station the Indians on board could see soldiers on the platform. They jumped from the train and made off.

At the station it was found that the engine, with its driver and mate, had roared on into the distance and disappeared. Passepartout and two other passengers were also missing.

'The Indians have taken them!' sobbed Aouda.

'I shall find our brave Passepartout and the passengers,' Phileas Fogg told her. With a group of soldiers he set out after the Indians.

Aouda and Fix were waiting with the other passengers at the station when suddenly they heard a whistle. Then to their delight, they saw the engine coming back down the line. The driver told them that when he and his mate had come round, the Sioux chief had fled and the engine had come to a halt. They found that the fire in the engine had burned out. They re-lit the fire and had come back for the coaches. Once all the passengers were back on board the train, they would carry on to New York.

'But what about Mr Fogg and the missing passengers?' asked Aouda. 'Please don't leave without them,' she pleaded.

'They will have to get tomorrow's train,' the driver replied. Aouda refused to leave, and waited at the station as the train pulled out. Fix stayed with her, worried that he might still lose his bank-robber.

It was a long, cold night. As the sun rose on a snow-covered, icy scene, gun-shots were heard. Then, at last, a band of marching men appeared. Phileas Fogg was leading the group of lost passengers and soldiers! Soon Aouda was re-united with Fogg and Passepartout. She heard how Fogg had found Passepartout and the passengers fighting off the Sioux. The brave Passepartout had felled three Indians with his bare fists!

Fogg was angry that the train had left without them.

'I am twenty four hours late,' he said. 'I must be in New York on December the eleventh. The steamer sails for Liverpool at nine that evening!'

A man standing nearby heard this. He offered to take them on his wind-sledge, which ran on steel runners and had a large sail. Fogg gladly accepted, and soon the icy wind was carrying them, including Fix, fast over the frozen snow.

They came to a town where a train, bound for New York, was standing at the station. They boarded it and Fogg spoke to its driver, who ordered, 'full speed ahead'. The prairie and towns flashed by. Just after eleven in the evening, on December 11th, the train arrived

in New York. But they were too late. The
steamer for Liverpool had already sailed!

Determined not to be beaten, Fogg hurried
to the docks. There he found a small cargo
ship ready to sail.

'Where are you going?' he asked the
captain.

'Bordeaux, France,' was the reply.

'I'll pay you well to take me and three friends to Liverpool!' said Fogg.

'I sail for Bordeaux,' said the captain. 'I will take you there.'

'Agreed!' said Fogg.

An hour later, Fogg and his friends, together with Fix, sailed from New York. But Fogg had no intention of sailing to France. He had a plan. Secretly, he spoke to the sailors and paid them well. First, he had the captain locked in his cabin. Then Fogg took command of the ship.

All went well until a gale blew up. Fogg ordered the sails to be taken down. More coal was heaped on the furnaces to keep up the speed. Under black skies, huge waves crashed down on the little ship. Five days before he was due in London, Phileas Fogg was still in mid-Atlantic. The ship's engineer brought him bad news.

'The coal's almost gone, sir!' he gasped. 'We must slow down!'

'Not now,' replied Fogg. 'Full speed ahead!' Then he ordered the captain to be brought to the bridge. The captain raged like an unchained tiger.

'Pirate!' he stormed. 'You have stolen my ship!'

'Stolen?' said Fogg. 'I want to buy your ship.'

'I won't sell!' roared the captain.

'But I must burn her!' Fogg went on.

'Burn her!' gasped the captain. 'She's worth fifty thousand dollars!'

'I'll give you sixty thousand dollars,' Fogg said calmly. It was a bargain the captain could not refuse. He accepted, and joined in the fight to keep the little ship scudding along. When the coal was gone, they ripped up the decks and burned the wood. Everything that would burn was fed to the furnaces.

On the evening of December 20th they were south of Ireland.

Now, only twenty four hours remained for Phileas Fogg to get to London and win his bet. They landed in Cork harbour, then a fast train took them to Dublin where they took the boat to Liverpool.

Fogg felt safe as he stepped ashore at Liverpool. He knew he could reach London in six hours, and there were nine hours left.

At that moment, Phileas Fogg felt a heavy hand on his shoulder.

'I arrest you in the Queen's name!' said Fix, the detective.

Passepartout raised his fist, but policemen grabbed his arms, and Fogg was put in a cell in the Customs House.

Poor Passepartout told Aouda the whole story. He blamed himself for everything. If only he had told his master about Fix!

Phileas Fogg sat in his cell watching the seconds tick away. It seemed impossible that, on the very last day, he could fail. At thirty-three minutes past two, the door of his cell was flung open, and Passepartout, Aouda and Fix burst in.

'Sir,' stammered Fix, 'I was mistaken! The real robber was caught three days ago! You are free!'

Phileas Fogg got up slowly. He walked calmly up to Fix, staring into the detective's eyes. Then with one swift blow he knocked Fix out.

'Well hit, sir!' laughed Passepartout.

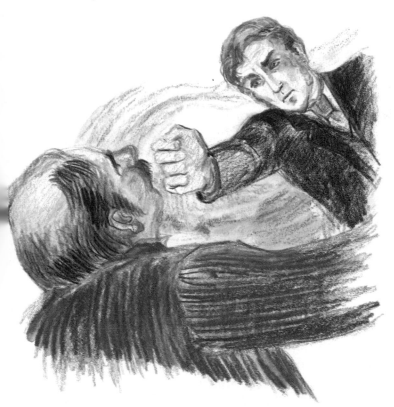

Fogg ordered a special train which set off for London at top speed. But as it puffed into the station, the clocks of London showed it was ten minutes to nine. After travelling around the world, Phileas Fogg was just five minutes late. He had lost his bet.

Sadly, the three travellers returned to Fogg's house. Few words were spoken. They all knew that Phileas Fogg was ruined.

Passepartout, who blamed himself, went to Aouda's room. 'Madam,' he pleaded, 'please try to comfort Mr Fogg. He sends me away.'

When Phileas Fogg came to talk to Aouda about his plans for her, she told him, 'If you had not saved me, you would have had time to spare.'

'You are safe,' said Fogg. 'It doesn't matter what happens to me. I have no family to care about me.'

'A pity,' sighed Aouda. 'Trouble is easier to bear when it is shared.'

'So they say,' said Fogg.

'Then share your troubles with me!' said Aouda. 'Will you have me as your wife?'

'With all my heart I will!' answered Fogg. At once, he sent for Passepartout and told him to arrange the wedding.

'When will it be, sir?' he asked. He was delighted at the news. 'Tomorrow, Monday!' replied the happy Phileas Fogg.

As fast as his legs could carry him, Passepartout ran to the vicar's house. 'Please, sir,' he said breathlessly, 'will you arrange the marriage of my master, Mr Phileas Fogg, for tomorrow, Monday?'

'No, no, my man,' said the vicar. 'Tomorrow

is Sunday, not Monday. It's Saturday today.'

'Today is Saturday?' gasped Passepartout. To the vicar's amazement, Passepartout rushed out of the room and into the street. Bursting into Fogg's room, Passepartout cried, 'Hurry, master! We were wrong! Today is Saturday! There are still ten minutes left for you to win your bet!'

Fogg was stunned. He couldn't have made a mistake! He had counted every day. Then he realised that, as he had travelled east, he

should have altered his watch. Every fifteen degrees he travelled, he should have put his watch back one hour. In going round the world he had gained twenty four hours – a whole day! He sprang into action.

On the evening of Saturday, December 21st, the group of friends met at the Reform Club. It was Fogg's eightieth day. They had had no recent news of his travels, and no one knew if he was still alive.

'It's twenty past eight,' said one. 'The last train from Liverpool has already arrived. He can't get here now!'

'Not so fast,' said another. 'Phileas Fogg is a very exact man. We are not safe until a quarter to nine.'

The minutes ticked away. The second hand swept away the last minute. The clock began to chime the third quarter. The door burst open.

'Here I am, gentlemen,' said Phileas Fogg. Behind him was an excited crowd.

Through every kind of danger, he had travelled around the world in eighty days. He had won his race against time. He had won his bet. Better still, he had found Aouda. Phileas Fogg was the happiest man in the world!

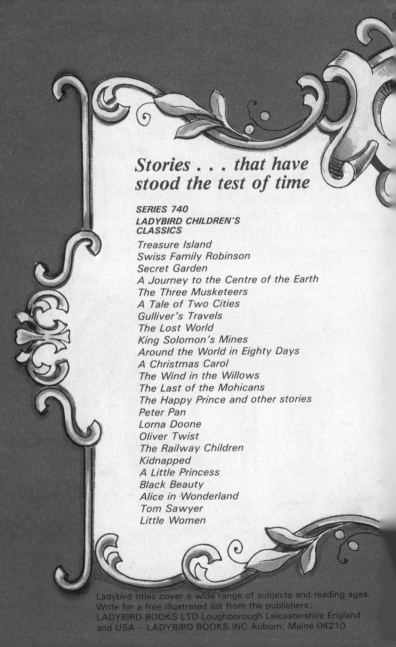

Stories . . . that have stood the test of time

SERIES 740
LADYBIRD CHILDREN'S
CLASSICS

Treasure Island
Swiss Family Robinson
Secret Garden
A Journey to the Centre of the Earth
The Three Musketeers
A Tale of Two Cities
Gulliver's Travels
The Lost World
King Solomon's Mines
Around the World in Eighty Days
A Christmas Carol
The Wind in the Willows
The Last of the Mohicans
The Happy Prince and other stories
Peter Pan
Lorna Doone
Oliver Twist
The Railway Children
Kidnapped
A Little Princess
Black Beauty
Alice in Wonderland
Tom Sawyer
Little Women

Ladybird titles cover a wide range of subjects and reading ages.
Write for a free illustrated list from the publishers:
LADYBIRD BOOKS LTD Loughborough Leicestershire England
and USA — LADYBIRD BOOKS INC Auburn, Maine 04210